The extraordinary tales of

 Alice Moon

Finding Lost Treasures

Jo Brothers

Illustrated by Lovee

The Extraordinary Tales of Queenie Alice Moon - Finding Lost Treasures

Second Printing, 2015
Text and Artwork Copyright © 2015 Jo Brothers
ISBN 978-0-9941093-1-6

Published by:
Perpetuity Media
PO Box 4444
Shortland Street
Auckland
New Zealand 1140

www.perpetuitymedia.com

Published in New Zealand

Printed in the United States of America

Everyone has
extraordinary tales to tell.

This book is dedicated to

you.

Every morning Queenie Alice Moon was woken up by a stunning peacock called Angelo who blew a golden trumpet to wake up everyone in the Kingdom. Queenie would then get out of bed and quickly get ready for the day ahead. She did not like to sit still.

However this morning when Angelo blew the trumpet Queenie woke up and something was wrong. She looked around and saw Moonbeam her Unicorn standing at the edge of her bed asleep on his feet, Pugnatius the Pug asleep next to her and Yang the Dragon asleep by her bedroom door.

They were her magical royal guardians who guarded and protected Queenie all the time.

Queenie sneezed, and coughed and soon everyone in the room was awake.

"Queenie, have you got a case of snake fever?", asked Pugnatius as he felt her temperature with his paw. Queenie had recently been in close contact with the vile Admiral Serpentine, head of the evil flying snake army, while on her way to visit Bluebelle the Fairy Queen.

"No! I simply can not be sick!", Queenie said with a defiant tone, as she attempted to sit up quickly. Immediately she felt dizzy and she could see small evil flying snakes flying around in circles in front of her eyes.

"Oh no, I'm seeing ugly small flying snakes!", she gasped as she closed her eyes.

Yang the Dragon opened the door, calling for the Royal Nurse, Harmony. "Harmony, Harmony, please come quickly, we suspect Queenie has a case of snake fever."

Nurse Harmony had been with the Moon family for generations and she like them was also part-Angel and had studied nursing with Bluebelle the Fairy Queen.

Harmony arrived in Queenie's room in a cloud of magical green vapour, saying "Queenie my darling, let me take a look at you!", as she rushed to Queenie's bedside.

"Oh, yes it is a severe case of snake fever, I can see the little terrors flying around as clear as day. Bed rest for you Queenie and you must drink eight cups of Angelica potion every day for the next three days and hold this magic pink crystal of love. Thank goodness Bluebelle has just made a fresh supply of Angelica potion".

Harmony tucked Queenie into bed and asked for Yang, Pugnatius and Moonbeam to leave the room and summoned Queenie's parents.

Queenie turned to look at her parents. A tear slid down Queenie's face, she could not bear the thought of spending any time at all in bed and she did not want to be unwell, particularly with disgusting snake fever.

"Queenie, you will be perfectly well very soon, take this time to rest, the universe must want you to rest now and to rejuvenate", said Queenie's mother, Queen Arabella.

"Your mother is right Queenie.", said King Leo. "Just take a nice sip of Angelica potion and you will be able to rest and sleep it off."

Queenie took the goblet and drank every last drop. She wanted to be perfectly healthy now and always.

Queenie lay back in her bed and closed her eyes, she was feeling very tired and her bed was very warm and comforting. She could hear Pugnatius snoring in the distance.

Queenie opened her eyes and could not believe what she saw, beautiful large crystals everywhere! Somehow she was in the old underground Crystal Fields, she knew this from the old history books she loved to read.

The entrance to the Crystal Fields had been lost during the great evil flying snake war. A thousand years ago, Spectrum was under attack from the evil flying snakes despite the energetic protective force fields.

Spectrum was attacked and nearly destroyed by Lord Serpentine and his hideous army. Lord Serpentine was a distant relative of the current leader Admiral Serpentine.

It was during this time that the Heavenly Government established the undercover Angels to protect all the Kingdoms, Realms and people around the Worlds so that this disgusting attack could never happen again.

That was when Queenie's family joined the Heavenly Government as undercover Angels.

Queenie started walking deeper into the cave, moving towards a large room filled with crystals.

Queenie looked down and saw water running along the bottom of the cave. She saw glowworms on the walls glowing in a golden hue so she was able to see her way as she walked toward a glowing green light.

Queenie wondered to herself where Pugnatius, Moonbeam and Yang were and how she had gotten to the Crystal Fields. She was determined to keep moving forward and moved towards the light to discover what had happened.

As Queenie turned the last corner she let out a gasp! She could not believe her eyes, here before her was the Ice Palace. A Palace larger than her parent's Palace and now deep underground.

History had taught Spectrum that the Ice Palace, home to the Crystal Elves, had been destroyed over a thousand years ago in the great evil flying snake war.

"Can I help you?" asked a man in a melodious voice. Queenie felt a nervous shiver run down her back, as she turned to see a tall translucent Crystal Elf, with golden hair and Princely robes. Queenie gasped, the Crystal Elves had not been seen in over a thousand years.

"Hi, I'm Queenie from Spectrum, the land above this cave" she said doing a curtsey. "Nice to meet you Queenie, I am Captain Zinc and I look after the Crystal Fields. We are not aware of any other inhabitants of this world, so seeing you is quite a shock but a pleasant shock. Let me guide you around, I will show you the Mineral Gardens and take you to the Sword in the Stone, the most power crystal and our guardian.", explained Captain Zinc.

Captain Zinc told Queenie the amazing history of how the Crystal Elves spun crystal into building materials to rebuild the Ice Palace and that the Mineral Gardens grew beautiful gem stones that glowed in the walls of the Palace providing heat and energy.

Queenie and Captain Zinc had walked all around the giant Crystal Palace and were now in a large room. She looked up through the clear crystal roof and saw water above with the most beautiful water roses floating serenely. A strange thought raced through Queenie's mind, something about the roses.

"I spend most of my time in the Engine Room, thinking of ways to improve life for us down here. I remember the stories of our ancient history, where my people spent many wonderful years living with the fairies above ground and I wish they were all still alive.", Captain Zinc said with a tear in his eye.

"They are alive Captain Zinc, the fairies are alive!", Queenie said with excitement. Captain Zinc smiled at Queenie, as she felt her arm being tugged. She turned her head to see Pugnatius shaking her arm. What was going on, was she back in her bedroom? Queenie sat up quickly remembering her adventure with Captain Zinc and the glowing crystals.

"Queenie you have slept for three days! Nurse Harmony knew you would hate to have little doses of Angelica potion so she gave it to you all at once!", Pugnatius said smiling.

"I have just had the most real dream, I am sure it was a message, please get my parents!", Queenie said as she kissed Pugnatius on his head.

Moonbeam gave Queenie's parents the secret signal that they should return to Queenie immediately and both King Leo and Queen Arabella appeared in Queenie's bedroom.

"The Crystal Palace and the Crystal Elves are alive! I have been there to visit them in my dream. They have used Elf technology to rebuild their world but they miss the fairies very much and did not know that we had survived the great evil flying snake war.", Queenie said excitedly.

"Okay Queenie, we know that messages come to us in dreams, so we will follow up on this dream of yours. Where shall we look for the entrance to their World?", King Leo asked.

Queenie closed her eyes and thought for a moment. "Roses! Where Fairy Rosa Amorosa lives those flowers were floating in her lake. The entrance must be at the bottom of the lake!", Queenie said with certainty.

Rosa Amorosa made beautiful perfumes and candles for all the Kingdoms and her cottage on the lake was always covered in water roses that volunteered to be used in perfumes and re-growing candles.

There was always an energy of happiness and mystery at the lake.

"I will go to Rosa's immediately and I promise you I will investigate this Queenie", King Leo said.

"Thank you and please say hello to Captain Zinc for me.", Queenie said as she waved her father goodbye. Queenie wanted to go with her father, however she knew she needed to stay and rest at home and be a good patient.

King Leo and his team of men arrived at Fairy Rosa Amorosa's cottage and he told Rosa the story of Queenie's dream. He asked for Rosa's blessing to search the bottom of the lake to see if the Crystal Palace lay beneath the lake.

Rosa happily agreed. She talked to her water roses on the lake and they all parted to the side of the lake to help King Leo's investigation.

A water fairy named Jack had been called in from another realm and was soon ready to dive to the bottom of the lake and to report back on what he found. Jack took a deep breath of air and dove deep down into the lake.

Fairy Rosa Amorosa and King Leo waited and waited and waited. Having patience is a great quality for a person to have, as usually the best things in life take time.

Bubbles began appearing on the surface of the lake and Jack burst up through the water and jumped up to lie on the floating wooden pontoon gasping for air.

Once again King Leo and Fairy Rosa Amorosa waited.

Jack got his breathe back saying, "Queenie is right, the Crystal Palace is down there. I made contact with Captain Zinc and we have a plan to build a bridge between the Worlds."

Over the next few hours hundreds of fairies, angels, bumble bees and butterflies worked to create a bridge between the Worlds.

They left the lake as it was and special crystals were used to cut a staircase from Crystal Fields to open out at the far side of the lake near the Emerald fields.

Humming birds spread the news to everyone in Spectrum that the Crystal Elves had been found alive and well. Great celebrations went on across the lands as everyone celebrated the reunion of the Crystal Elves with the people of Spectrum.

Crystal Elves were seen running in the long grass, smelling the flowers and playing with their friends the fairies. Similarly the fairies loved the Crystal Palace and all the Crystal medicine the Crystal Elves had developed and were seen being mischievous in the Crystal Palace.

Queenie was in the gardens in her rope swing covered in roses, so happy that her getting sick with snake fever and being dosed up on Angelica potion had led her on a journey that resulted in unlocking an entire World that had been hidden for thousands of years.

Queenie thought for a moment, thank goodness I caught snake fever that led to my dream and that led to such happiness.

Sometimes, when life sends us to bed to rest, it is so that life can give us even bigger gifts than we have had ever before.

Whatever happens to us is meant to happen and whatever happens to us is in our best interest.

About Jo

Jo has a passion for storytelling and writing that started when she was a young girl and continues to this very day. She has a vivid imagination and loves creating new worlds and wonderful characters that burst into life with valour and flamboyance such as Queenie Alice Moon and Nano the Robot.

She equally writes intriguing novelettes with quirky, eccentric characters that are weaved into supernatural themes and in her soon to be released books series, Immortales Excelsus she writes about an ordinary, thoroughly bored teen, Sabra Leon, who discovers she and her family are not so ordinary and that their history has more than a few secrets that date back to the dawn of time.

"Thanks for visiting, happy imagining! "

Please keep in touch with me at www.jobrothers.com

Jo lives in Auckland, New Zealand with her husband Sean, in a home filled with books and imagination.